Once Upon a now

EGMONT
We bring stories to life

First published in Great Britain in 2015 by Egmont UK Limited
The Yellow Building, 1 Nicholas Road, London W11 4AN

Written by Mara Alperin
Designed by Jeannette O'Toole

© 2015 Disney Enterprises, Inc.

ISBN 978 1 4052 8013 6
62961/1
Printed in Italy

be the change
you want to see

Contents

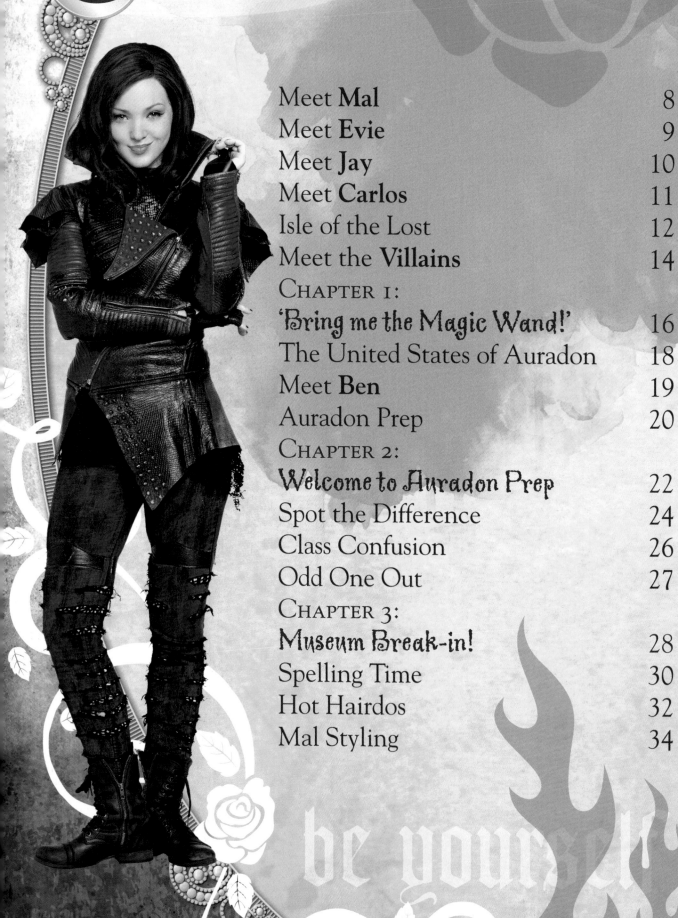

Change for the better

be yourself

Meet Mal

Sixteen-year-old Mal is the leader of her group of friends. Mal wants to be **wicked**, just like her mother Maleficent!

Mal

FACT FILE

MOTHER: Maleficent

LIKES: Being EVIL!

DISLIKES: Goodness, swimming

Meet Evie

The daughter of the **Evil Queen**, Evie dreams of finding a **prince** to marry ... and she never goes anywhere without her TIARA! Her best friend is Mal.

EVIE

MOTHER: Evil Queen

LIKES: Sewing, mirrors

DISLIKES: Bad hair days!

FACT FILE

Meet Jay

Jay is charming, HANDSOME and athletic ... but he's also sneaky and mischievous! He steals things for his father, Jafar, to sell in his shop.

FACT FILE

FATHER: Jafar

LIKES: Thievery

DISLIKES: Sharing

Meet Carlos

Carlos might be tech-savvy, but he's TERRIFIED of DOGS! His mother, **Cruella**, told him that dogs eat boys who don't behave! Carlos' best friends are **Jay**, **Mal** and **Evie**.

MOTHER: Cruella de Vil

LIKES: Technology

DISLIKES: Dogs

FACT FILE

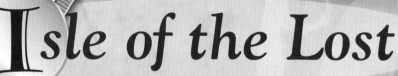

Isle of the Lost

Once upon a time, after the Beast married Belle, he united the kingdoms and became **KING** of the United States of Auradon. **King Beast** rounded up all the evil villains and their sidekicks, and BANISHED them to the **Isle of the Lost.**

Then one day, King Beast's son, **Ben**, decided the children of the villains deserved a SECOND CHANCE. And so he issued an **OFFICIAL PROCLAMATION** …

'The children on the Isle of the Lost should be given a chance to live in Auradon.'

AURADON

Wicked Wordsearch

Can you find all **10** words hidden in the square?

BADNESS
CRUELLA
ENEMIES
EVIL QUEEN
JAFAR
MAGIC MIRROR
MALEFICENT
REVENGE
SPELL BOOK
VILLAIN

M	A	L	E	F	I	C	E	N	T	X
T	I	W	V	I	L	L	A	I	N	P
M	A	G	I	C	M	I	R	R	O	R
C	O	K	L	Z	E	K	O	B	L	E
S	R	A	Q	A	R	A	F	A	J	V
E	N	U	U	P	B	L	H	D	M	E
I	E	L	E	A	S	O	I	N	P	N
M	E	R	E	L	W	X	K	E	S	G
E	Q	W	N	B	L	K	W	S	A	E
N	W	A	P	K	W	A	C	S	O	V
E	S	P	E	L	L	B	O	O	K	P

Words read forwards, backwards, up, down and diagonally!

Secret Code

Use the key to decipher the message.

E   G   I   L   N   O   V

Answers on page 68.

Meet the Villains

NAME: **Maleficent**
NEMESIS: Sleeping Beauty
FAVOURITE QUOTE:

'When I was your age, I was cursing entire kingdoms!'

NAME: **Evil Queen**
NEMESIS: Snow White
FAVOURITE QUOTE:

'Who is the fairest of them all?'

NAME: Jafar

NEMESIS: Aladdin

FAVOURITE QUOTE:

'There's no team in i.'

NAME: Cruella de Vil

NEMESIS: Every squeaky Dalmatian that escaped her clutches

FAVOURITE QUOTE:

'That puppy would make the perfect coat!'

CHAPTER 1

'Bring Me the Magic Wand!'

Maleficent, the **Mistress of Darkness and All Evil**, had a plan. A horrible, fiendish plan – a plan fit for the most **POWERFUL** and **WICKED** fairy in the world.

She gathered her fellow villains **Cruella, Jafar** and **Evil Queen** together in her dark and dusty flat. Then they sat down their children to explain.

'There's an official proclamation from the **KING**,' Maleficent said, reading from the scroll. 'You four have been chosen to go to **AURADON PREP.**'

'This is about **WORLD DOMINATION!**'

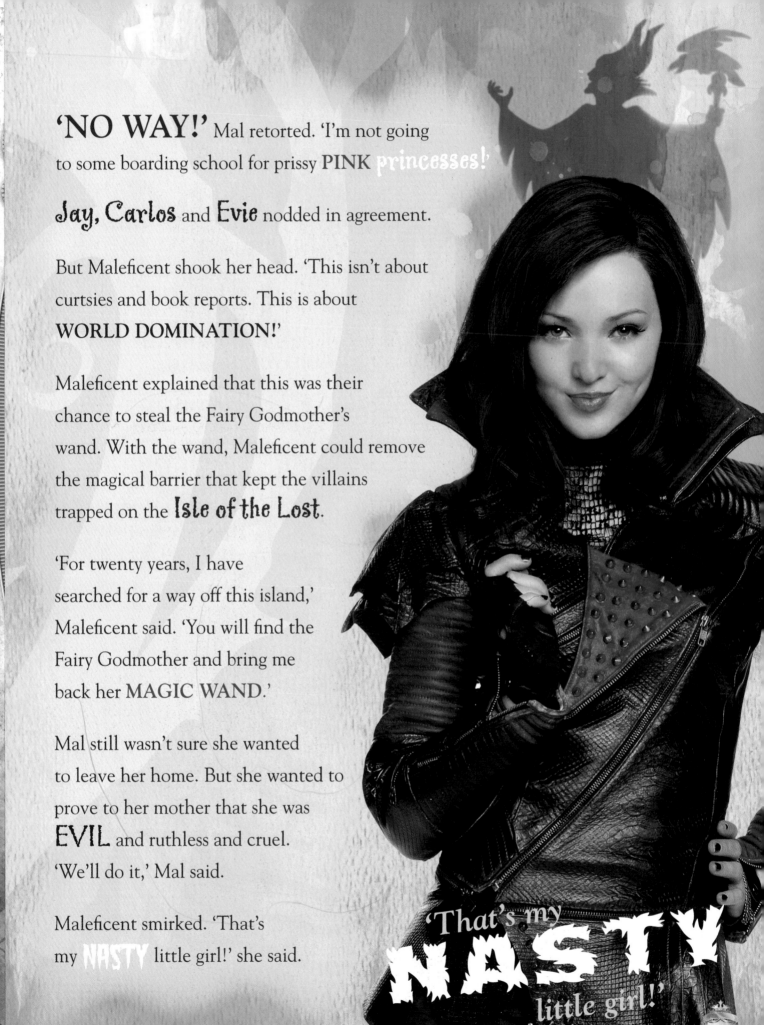

'NO WAY!' Mal retorted. 'I'm not going to some boarding school for prissy **PINK** princesses!'

Jay, Carlos and **Evie** nodded in agreement.

But Maleficent shook her head. 'This isn't about curtsies and book reports. This is about **WORLD DOMINATION!'**

Maleficent explained that this was their chance to steal the Fairy Godmother's wand. With the wand, Maleficent could remove the magical barrier that kept the villains trapped on the **Isle of the Lost**.

'For twenty years, I have searched for a way off this island,' Maleficent said. 'You will find the Fairy Godmother and bring me back her **MAGIC WAND**.'

Mal still wasn't sure she wanted to leave her home. But she wanted to prove to her mother that she was **EVIL** and ruthless and cruel. 'We'll do it,' Mal said.

Maleficent smirked. 'That's my **NASTY** little girl!' she said.

'That's my **NASTY** little girl!'

Auradon Prep

MOTHER:
Fairy Godmother

LIKES: *Friendship*

DISLIKES: *Her hair*

Jane

Meet Audrey

PARENTS:
Sleeping Beauty and Prince Phillip

LIKES: *Cheerleading*

DISLIKES: *Mal and the other villains' kids*

Audrey

'NO WAY!' Mal retorted. 'I'm not going to some boarding school for prissy PINK princesses!'

Jay, Carlos and Evie nodded in agreement.

But Maleficent shook her head. 'This isn't about curtsies and book reports. This is about WORLD DOMINATION!'

Maleficent explained that this was their chance to steal the Fairy Godmother's wand. With the wand, Maleficent could remove the magical barrier that kept the villains trapped on the Isle of the Lost.

'For twenty years, I have searched for a way off this island,' Maleficent said. 'You will find the Fairy Godmother and bring me back her MAGIC WAND.'

Mal still wasn't sure she wanted to leave her home. But she wanted to prove to her mother that she was EVIL and ruthless and cruel. 'We'll do it,' Mal said.

Maleficent smirked. 'That's my NASTY little girl!' she said.

'That's my NASTY little girl!'

17

The United States of Auradon

The **United States** of **Auradon** is a beautiful kingdom, but only **HEROES** and their children can live there! Mal and her friends are the first children of **VILLAINS** allowed in!

Help Mal and her friends through the maze to Auradon Prep!

START

FINISH

AURADON

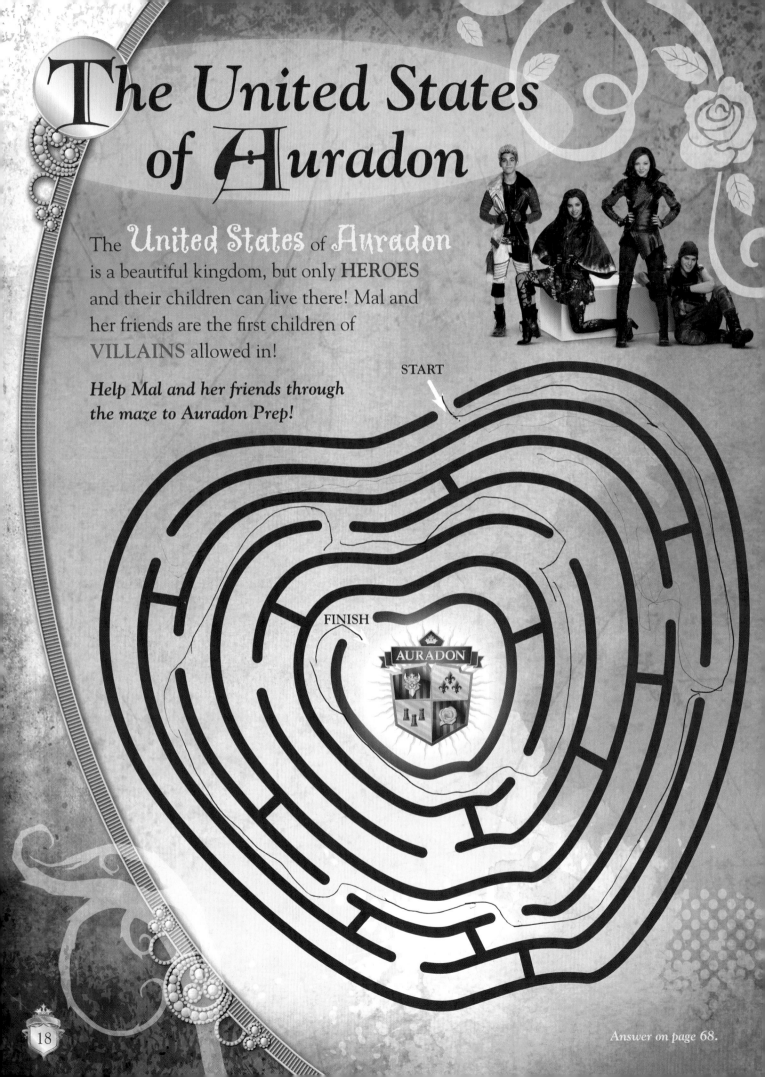

Answer on page 68.

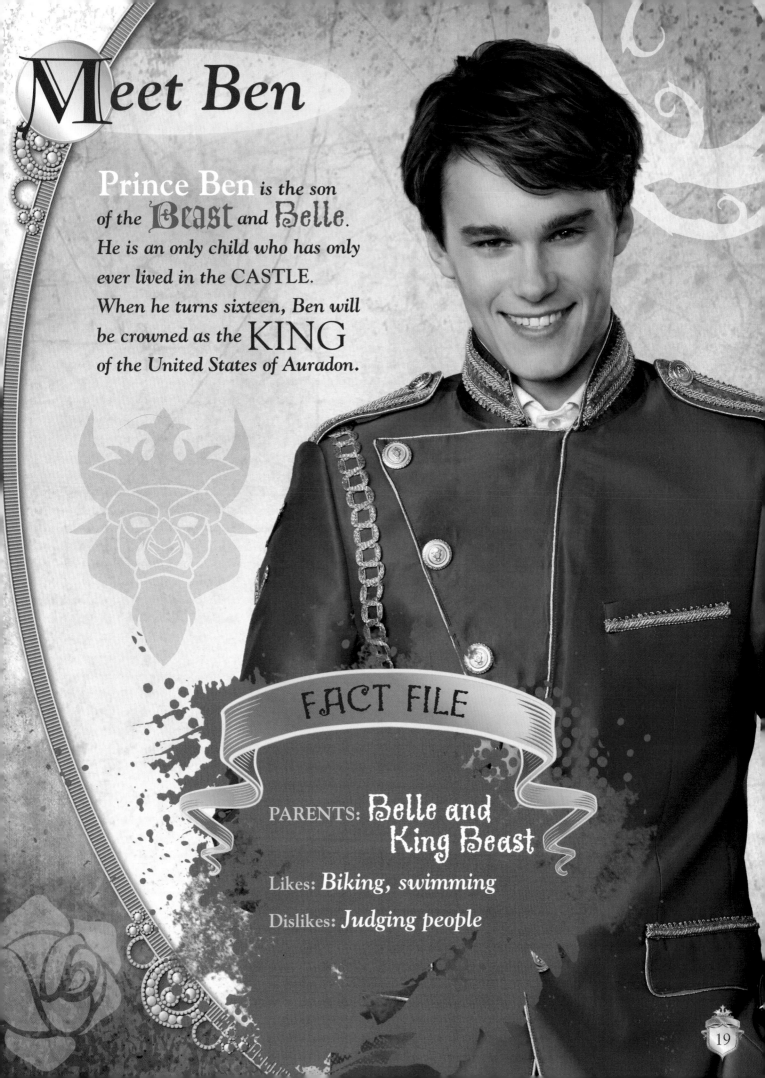

Meet Ben

Prince Ben *is the son of the* 𝕭east *and* 𝕭elle. *He is an only child who has only ever lived in the* CASTLE. *When he turns sixteen, Ben will be crowned as the* KING *of the United States of Auradon.*

FACT FILE

PARENTS: **Belle and King Beast**

Likes: *Biking, swimming*

Dislikes: *Judging people*

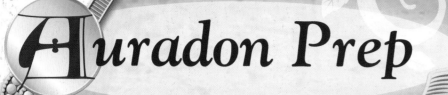 Auradon Prep

MOTHER:
Fairy Godmother

LIKES: *Friendship*

DISLIKES: *Her hair*

Jane

Meet Audrey

PARENTS:
Sleeping Beauty and Prince Phillip

LIKES: *Cheerleading*

DISLIKES: *Mal and the other villains' kids*

Audrey

PARENTS:
Cinderella and
Prince Charming

LIKES: *Sports, looking handsome*

DISLIKES: *Studying*

Chad

MOTHER:
Mulan

LIKES: *Chocolate chip cookies*

DISLIKES: *Sad stories*

Lonnie

FATHER: **Dopey**

LIKES: Marching band

DISLIKES: Being picked on

Doug

CHAPTER 2

Welcome to Auradon Prep

Mal and her friends arrived at Auradon Prep. Mal nearly gagged when she saw the sign out front:

'Welcome to Auradon Prep. Goodness doesn't get any better.'

A smiling woman stepped out to meet them. 'I'm Fairy Godmother, the Headmistress at Auradon Prep,' she said, bowing elegantly.

'THE Fairy Godmother?' Mal asked. 'As in Bibbidi-Bobbidi-Boo? I didn't recognise you without your magic wand.'

The Fairy Godmother laughed. 'That was a long time ago,' she said. 'At Auradon Prep, we believe that REAL magic is in books and learning! I don't use the wand anymore – it's at the Museum of Cultural History.'

'I'm **Fairy Godmother,** the Headmistress at **AURADON PREP.'**

Before Mal could respond,
one of the students stepped forwards.
'I'm Ben,' he said. 'It's great to finally meet you all!'

'Prince Ben?' Evie asked. She curtsied and fluttered her eyelashes.

'Let me take you on a tour of Auradon Prep,' Ben said. He showed Mal and her friends the gardens and the halls, sharing information about the school and its history. Then he introduced them to Doug, who was the son of Dopey the Dwarf, and Audrey, the daughter of Sleeping Beauty.

'I'll see you in class tomorrow,'
Ben told Mal with a grin.

Ben was very handsome, and he kept smiling at Mal. But Mal couldn't stop thinking about the Fairy Godmother's wand. Somehow, they would have to break into the museum!

Spot the Difference

These two pictures at **Auradon Prep** may look the same,
but there are eight differences in picture 2. Can you spot them all?

1

Tick an **apple** each time you spot a difference.

2

Class Confusion

Mal's Auradon Prep schedule has some classes missing. **Can you use the clues below to fill in the timetable?**

TIME	CLASS
8am-9am	
9am-10am	
10am-11am	FREE TIME
11am-12pm	
12pm-1pm	LUNCH
1pm-2pm	
2pm-3pm	

CLASSES

* History of Woodsmen
* Bad Fairies
* Grammar
* Mathematics
* History of Auradon

AURADON

CLUES

1. History of Auradon comes right after the free time.
2. History of Woodsmen is in the afternoon.
3. Mal goes straight from Bad Fairies to Grammar class.
4. Mathematics isn't right before lunch, or right after lunch.

Answers on page 68.

Odd One Out

Mal and Evie are revising together.
Can you spot which of these six pictures is the odd one out?

a

b

c

d

e

f

Answers on page 68.

CHAPTER 3

Museum Break-in!

Later that night, Mal gathered Evie, Jay and Carlos. 'Now's our chance to steal the wand, while everyone is sleeping,' Mal whispered.

The four friends crept out of their dormitories, and made their way to the Museum of Cultural History.

At the museum, a tall guard was standing at the entrance.

'How are we going to get past the guard?' asked Carlos.

Peeking through the window, Mal saw her mother's old spinning wheel. She had an idea. She took out her spell book and chanted:

'Prick the finger, prick it deep.
Send my enemy off to sleep.'

In a daze, the guard wandered over and touched the spinning wheel. He yawned and fell right asleep.

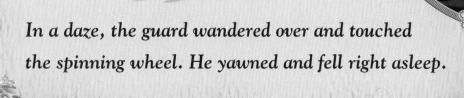

'Now's our chance to steal the WAND, while everyone is sleeping.'

'Nice one!' said Jay.

Mal tiptoed into the museum, with her friends right behind her. After a bit of searching, she spotted the magic wand, resting in a display case. 'Over here!' she called.

But as Jay reached to grab the wand ... CRACK! He was thrown back by a giant shock. The wand was protected by a force field and a very loud siren!

The alarm had woken the guard in the lobby. 'Who's there?' he bellowed.

Mal and her friends ducked behind a table ... and sprinted out the door when the guard was looking the other way.

Mal was so disappointed. Now she would need to come up with a PLAN B!

Spelling Time

Maleficent gave Mal her old spell book so she can practise using magic.

Cross out all the capital letters to reveal Mal's museum spell.

DmEaSgCiEcN

DsApNiTnSdDlEeS, CdEoN

DnAoNtT SlDiEnSgCeErN.

DmAaNkTeS DmEyS

CvEiNcDtAiNmT

SpDrEiScCkE NaD

AfNiTnSgDeErS.

Write out the spell below.

_____

_____

_____

_____

_____

_____

Mal also uses magic to give her classmates cool, new hairstyles!

Now cross out all the 'x's' to reveal Mal's hairstyle spell.

xbxxewxarxe, fxorswxeaxxr, rxepxxlaxcxe thxxe xolxd wxixth bxxranxxd-nxexw hxaixrx.

Write out the spell below.

_____

_____

_____

_____

If I had a spell book, this is the spell I would cast:

_____

_____

_____

_____

Answers on page 68.

hot Hairdos

Mal's spells transform Jane's and Lonnie's hair. Her friends love their new looks!

Jane

Before

After

Lonnie

Before

After

What's your hair accessory?

Tick your favourite choices to reveal which
hair accessory would best complement your style.

1. How would you describe your style?

a) casual ☐   b) unique ☐   c) classy ☐

2. What do you wear when you go out with your friends?

a) skinny jeans ☐   b) mini skirt ☐   c) pencil skirt ☐

3. How would your friends describe you?

a) laid-back ☐   b) outgoing ☐

c) sophisticated ☐

Count how many a's, b's and c's you scored!

Mostly a's

Your confident
and casual style shows
off your natural beauty.
You hair accessory is
a **headband**! Simple
but pretty, headbands
add a fun splash
of colour.

Mostly b's

Your style is creative,
bold and original. A
hairbow is perfect
for you! They come in
all colours and patterns,
so you can create a
unique look that's all
your own.

Mostly c's

You always look
sensational, even if
it means taking a while
to get ready. Tie a **scarf**
in your hair, for
an elegant,
glamorous look.

Mal's classmates LOVE her style! It's **punk-rock,** and seriously COOL!

With Mal's UNIQUE look, she really stands out from the CROWD!

MAL

Studded bracelets bring Mal's look together.

/10

This asymmetric hemline adds extra flair!

/10

Mal's cool, edgy tee with dragon-wing sleeves is one-of-a-kind!

/10

Give each item a score out of **10** for style. Which one is your **WINNER?**

High laces add a touch of punk to these classic black-leather ankle boots.

/10

/10

Mal's green, ripped denim jeans are customised with leather knee patches.

CHAPTER 4

The Love Spell

Back at school, Mal had another idea. The Fairy Godmother would bring her wand to Prince Ben's Coronation. Ben would be sitting in the very front row … with his parents and his girlfriend.

If Mal was Ben's girlfriend, she would get to sit next to Ben. She would be right by the WAND!

In her spell book, Mal found a recipe for chocolate chip cookies – with a Love Spell! Evie, Jay and Carlos helped her mix all the ingredients together. Then Mal recited:

'Crush his heart
with an iron glove,
By making him
a slave to LOVE.'

The next morning Mal offered a cookie to Ben. She wondered what would happen next.

But the spell worked a little TOO well! Ben stood in front of the entire school and sang a love song to Mal. 'Give me an M, give me an A, give me an L!' Ben cheered. 'I love you, Mal, did I mention that?'

Give me an M, give me an A, give me a L!'

Then Ben invited Mal to go to the Coronation with him.

'Yes!' Mal said. 'I'll go with you!'

Mal and Ben would be up at the very front, just seconds away from the Fairy Godmother and her magic wand. Mal's plan to steal the wand so Maleficent could rule the kingdom was finally coming together!

Mal's Cookie Recipe

Make these yummy cookies just like Mal!

You will need ...

* 300g self-raising flour
* 30g cocoa powder
* 250g butter
* 125g caster sugar
* 200g chocolate chips or chocolate pieces

* a sieve
* a wooden spoon
* baking trays
* mixing bowls

Preparation time: 15 minutes
Cooking time: 10-15 minutes

Always ask an adult to help when using the oven.

1. Preheat oven to 160° C/ Fan oven 150° C/ Gas Mark 3. Grease the baking tray.

2. Sieve the flour and cocoa into a bowl.

3. Cream the butter and sugar together. Then stir the flour and cocoa into the mixture to make a dough.

4. Roll the dough into little balls, then put them on the baking trays with a little space between each one.

5. Flatten each biscuit with a spoon, and add the chocolate chips or chocolate pieces on top.

6. Ask an adult to put the cookies in the oven. Bake until the biscuits feel firm on the top (10-15 minutes).

7. Store the cookies on a cooling rack until they have cooled down enough to eat!

MAL

good as
gold

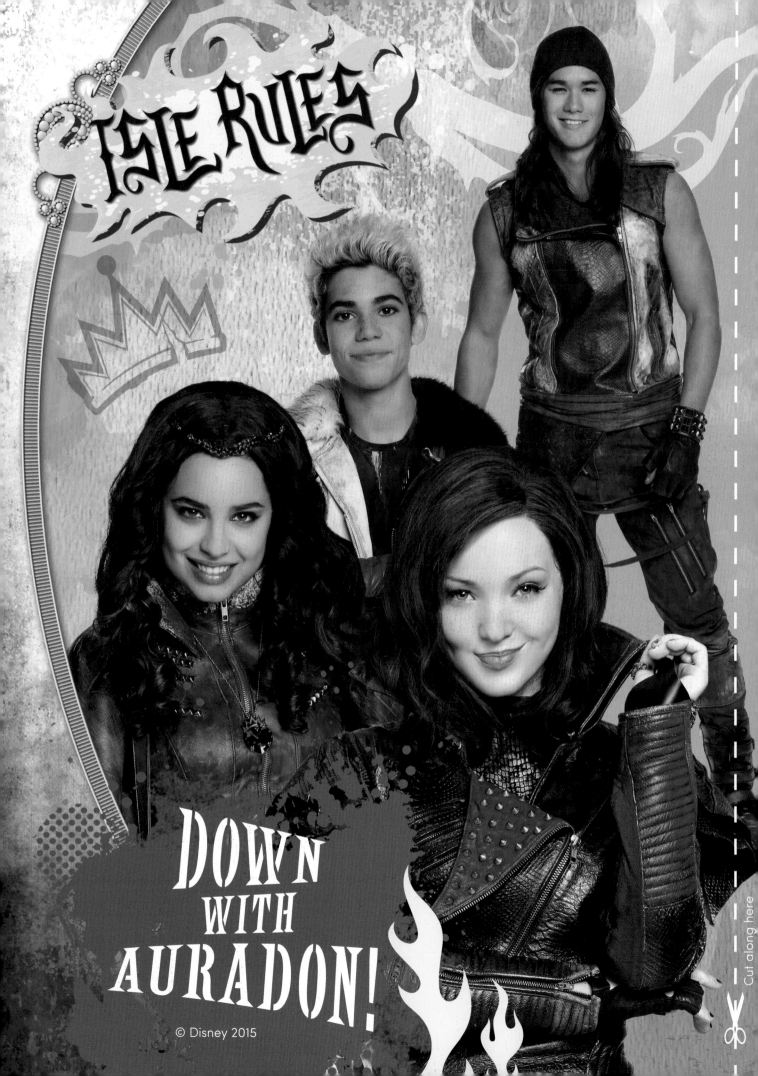

ISLE RULES

DOWN WITH AURADON!

© Disney 2015

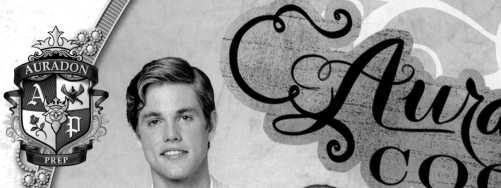

Change for the Better!

be the change
you want to see

On our BEST
behaviour!

Crazy Crossword

Read the clues to crack the crossword!

ACROSS
1. Cruella de Vil's son is called _ _ _ _ _ _ (6)
3. Chad's parents are Prince Charming and _ _ _ _ _ _ _ _ _ _ (10)
6. _ _ _ _ _ _ (6) is a cheerleader
7. Evil Queen gives Evie a magic _ _ _ _ _ _ (6)
9. Jane's mother is the Fairy _ _ _ _ _ _ _ _ _ (9)

DOWN
2. Mal casts spells using her _ _ _ _ _ _ _ _ _ (5, 4)
3. Ben will be crowned king at his _ _ _ _ _ _ _ _ _ _ (10)
4. King Beast is the king of _ _ _ _ _ _ _ (7)
5. Mal and her friends tried to break into the _ _ _ _ _ _ (6) of Cultural History
8. Carlos is afraid of _ _ _ _ (4)

Answers on page 68.

CHAPTER 5

The Enchanted Lake

Before the Coronation, Ben asked Mal out on a date. Mal was very nervous. She had never been on a date before!

Evie helped Mal get ready. 'You look fabulous!' she said. 'Don't worry, you're going to have a great time.'

Ben took Mal to the Enchanted Lake for a picnic. They ate strawberries and jelly doughnuts on a stone platform in the middle of the lake. Mal had never eaten strawberries or doughnuts before!

'Tell me something else about you,' Ben said. He took Mal's hand and held it in his.

'I love you, Mal.'

'My middle name is Bertha,' Mal said. 'That's my mom doing what she does best – being really EVIL!'

'My middle name is Florian,' Ben admitted. 'It's almost as bad.'

Mal started to laugh, and Ben looked deep into her eyes.

'I can see the goodness in you,'

Ben said. 'I love you, Mal.'

Mal didn't know what to think! She had actually started to like Ben ... but would he still be in love with her when the love spell ran out? And what would he say if he found out she was trying to steal the Fairy Godmother's wand?

Mal wondered if there really WAS goodness in her! She wasn't sure if she still wanted to carry out her mother's evil plan. What was she going to do?

Coronation Gowns

Evie is a top seamstress and designer. She helps her friends get ready for the Coronation.

Now design
your own spectacular
Coronation gown!

Why not try
a short gown for a
more fun look?

Don't forget
to add jewellery,
and maybe even
a tiara!

Coronation Puzzle

Mal and Evie are getting ready for the Coronation. Two of these pictures are identical. Can you work out which ones?

Answer on page 68.

King of Auradon

Ben is about to be crowned as King of Auradon! If you were the leader of Auradon, what new laws would you make?

AURADON

Proclamation 1

....
....
....
....

Proclamation 2

....
....
....
....

Proclamation 3

....
....
....

CHAPTER 6
Ben's Coronation

It was Coronation Day.

As Mal rode to the Coronation Hall, she gave Ben a cupcake to remove the love spell. She cared about Ben too much to force him to be in love with her.

'I really do love you, Mal.'

But Ben already knew about the love spell! The Enchanted Lake had washed away the spell, but not his true feelings for Mal. 'I really do love you, Mal,' he said.

As the Coronation started, Mal began to believe that things might actually turn out OK.

Suddenly, in a bolt of lightning, Maleficent appeared. She snatched the wand from the Fairy Godmother, and smiled at Mal. 'Now we can take over the kingdom and get rid of this Prince Ben and his silly royal family.'

'NO!' Mal shouted. 'My heart tells me that I want to be with Ben, not to rule the world with evil.'

Maleficent cackled cruelly. 'Enough!' she boomed.
'You all will regret this!' She transformed herself into
a HUGE, fire-breathing DRAGON!

Bravely, Mal stood by her friends and chanted
a powerful protection spell:

'The strength of evil is good as none,
When stands before four hearts as one.'

FLASH! Maleficent turned into a tiny lizard.

'You did it!' cried the Fairy Godmother. 'Maleficent shrank
to the size of the love in her heart. You've saved Auradon!'

Ben and Mal danced together, and everyone cheered. Mal smiled back.
Finally, even the daughter of Maleficent could have a happy ending!

'My heart tells me that I want to be with Ben, not to rule the world with evil.'

Spotlight on:

Mal & Ben

Mal didn't need a **love spell** after all – BEN liked her for who she was!

After Mal rescued Ben and all of Auradon from **Maleficent**, she realised she could have a **Happy Ending!**

1

Write three things you like best about Mal and Ben.

Mal and Ben go on their very first date!

2

3

Spotlight on:
Evie & Doug

Doug doesn't have any **royal blood**, but he helped Evie realise that she doesn't need a **PRINCE** to shine.

This **super-talented** girl can dance, sew and **ACE** her advanced Chemistry class!

Write three things you like best about Evie and Doug.

1

2

3

Evie and Doug enjoy lunch together!

Spotlight on:

Jay & the Knights

Jay had never been part of a team. Then he joined the Fighting Knights ... and they won the Tournament together! Celebrating with his team — and eating victory pizza — makes Jay very HAPPY.

Write three things you like best about Jay.

1

2

3

Jay and Coach talk about the next big game.

Spotlight on:
CARLOS & Dude

Carlos used to be AFRAID of all dogs. But then he met Dude, the Auradon Prep campus mutt. Now Carlos and Dude are best friends!

1

Write three things you like best about Carlos and Dude.

Dude is always there for Carlos!

2

3

Make a Student Planner

Now you can design your own
Auradon Prep student planner!

You will need ...

* Plain notebook or planner to decorate
* Scissors
* Glue
* Photos, stickers, old magazines to decorate
* Pens or crayons
* Clear nail polish

TIP:
Use an old newspaper on your table while you're working to keep it clean.

1. Cut out pictures and arrange on the cover of your planner. Glue them down to hold in place.

2. Add stickers and doodles.

3. Once your collage is in place, wait for it to dry. Then coat with a thin layer of clear nail polish as a sealer.

TIP: Why not add cut-outs of your favourite movies and bands as well?

my PLANNER

AURADON
A
P
PREP

Movie Quiz

How well do you know **Descendants?** Test your knowledge on this fun quiz!

1 What is Mal's motto?

a) 'Born to be royal'

b) 'Long live evil'

c) 'Everyone deserves a second chance'

2 What does Maleficent want Mal to steal?

a) Fairy Godmother's magic wand

b) Aladdin's lamp

c) Belle's enchanted rose

3 Where do Mal and her friends go to school?

a) Auradon Academy

b) Auradon Prep

c) Auradon College

4 What is the motto of Auradon Prep?

a) 'Villains beware!'

b) 'Believe in yourself!'

c) 'Goodness doesn't get any better that this!'

5 Who is Doug's father?

a) Dopey

b) Doc

c) Bashful

6 How does Mal sneak into the museum to look for the magic wand?

a) She uses an invisibility cloak

b) She disables the alarms with her tech skills

c) She puts a sleeping spell on the guard

7 What is the name of the dog that Carlos meets?

a) Rex

b) Spot

c) Dude

8 What does Mal put her love spell in?

a) lemon drizzle cakes

b) chocolate chip cookies

c) blueberry muffins

9 Where does Ben take Mal on their first date?

a) The Enchanted Lake

b) The Coronation Cathedral

c) The Auradon Prep Gardens

10 When Mal saves Auradon, what does Maleficent turn into?

a) a rat

b) a lizard

c) a beetle

Answer on page 68.

Who Said That?

Match these quotes to the characters who said them.

'Mirror, mirror, in my hand, where does Fairy Godmothers' wand stand?'

'My Dad is Prince Charming.'

Ben

'I'll show you around Auradon Prep. Heigh-ho!'

Evie

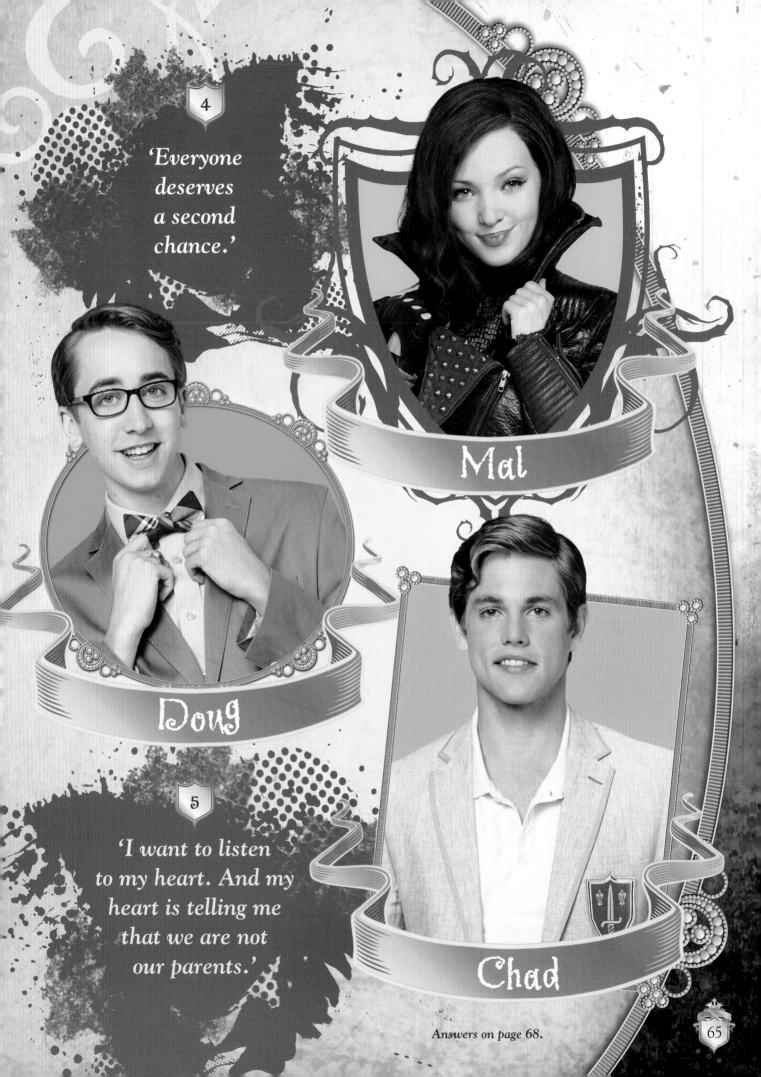

4

'Everyone deserves a second chance.'

Mal

Doug

5

'I want to listen to my heart. And my heart is telling me that we are not our parents.'

Chad

Answers on page 68.

Fairy Tale Facts

How well do you know your fairy tales? The facts below are muddled. Match each line with the correct answer!

Sneezy

pumpkin

apple

guest

spinning wheel

lamp

puppy

1. The Evil Queen gave Snow White a poisoned _____.

2. When Belle comes to the Beast's castle, the servants sing 'Be our _____!'

3. Cruella de Vil wanted to make a coat from a _____.

4. Fairy Godmother sent Cinderella to the ball in a coach made from a _____.

5. Jafar tried to steal Aladdin's magic _____.

6. The 7 dwarves are: Doc, Dopey, Sleepy, Happy, Grumpy, Bashful and _____.

7. Maleficent cursed Sleeping Beauty to prick her finger on a _____.

Answers on page 68.

Coronation Cathedral Colouring

Use your brightest pens or crayons to decorate the Coronation Hall stained glass window!

Answers

Page 13 Wicked Wordsearch

M	A	L	E	F	I	C	E	N	T	X
T	I	W	V	I	L	L	A	I	N	P
M	A	G	I	C	M	I	R	R	O	R
C	O	K	L	Z	E	K	O	B	L	E
S	R	A	Q	A	R	A	F	A	J	V
E	N	U	U	P	B	L	H	D	M	E
I	E	L	E	A	S	O	I	N	P	N
M	E	R	E	L	W	X	K	E	S	G
E	Q	W	N	B	L	K	W	S	A	E
N	W	A	P	K	W	A	C	S	O	V
E	S	P	E	L	L	B	O	O	K	P

Page 13 Secret Code
LONG LIVE EVIL

Page 18 The United States of Auradon

Page 24 Spot the Difference

Page 26 Class Confusion

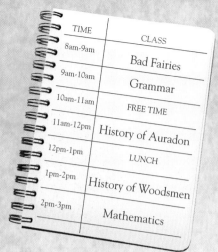

TIME	CLASS
8am-9am	Bad Fairies
9am-10am	Grammar
10am-11am	FREE TIME
11am-12pm	History of Auradon
12pm-1pm	LUNCH
1pm-2pm	History of Woodsmen
2pm-3pm	Mathematics

Page 27 Odd One Out
Picture c is the odd one out.

Page 30 Museum Spell
magic spindle, do not linger
make my victim prick a finger

Page 31 Hairstyle Spell
beware, forswear, replace
the old with brand-new hair

Page 43 Crazy Crossword

Page 48 Coronation Puzzle
Pictures a and d are the same.

Page 62 Movie Quiz
1. b, 2. a, 3. b, 4. c, 5. a, 6. c, 7. c, 8. b, 9. a, 10. b

Page 64 Who Said That?
1. Evie, 2. Chad, 3. Doug, 4. Ben, 5. Mal

Page 66 Fairy Tale Facts
1. apple, 2. guest, 3. puppy, 4. pumpkin,
5. lamp, 6. Sneezy, 7. spinning wheel

My Kingdom for a Kiss!